Diary of Harry Farter

Book 1

–Wimpy Fart–

You're awesome for reading

Wimpy Fart Books!

Thank You!

Table of Contents

Tuesday

Today is my 11th birthday! Everyone in my family is expecting me to give them the big news. They want me to discover that I'm not a Muggle, but a wizard with massive powers. I'm not going to lie, that's actually my birthday wish. Can you imagine what it feels like to be in a family where one of your cousins is famous all around the world?

Christina, my younger sister, wished me happy birthday at midnight and told me this year things will be different. She said not to worry about last year and to move on.

You see, last year on my 10th birthday I thought I was going to discover I'm a wizard. Unfortunately, things took a bad turn at school and I've had a hard time ever since. I still remember like it happened yesterday. I got to school and everyone was in the cafeteria before class. I was so sure I changed overnight because I felt different that morning. I had a tingling feeling all around my chest, stomach, and even my legs. I told my friends Paul and Shelly how I felt different that morning and they kept asking me to show them my power. They started chanting my name, "Harry! Harry! Harry!" Pretty soon the whole school was looking over to see what was going on.

Do you know what it's like to have everyone at school watching you, waiting for something spectacular to happen? I was nervous, and for some reason, until this day I'm not sure why, I climbed on top of the table and put my arms in the air so that everyone could see me. Even the teachers were watching at this point. The tingling feeling got stronger and stronger and it felt like I had a fireball in my stomach; I remember thinking to myself 'wow, I really am a wizard!'

I asked everyone to quiet down. I knew something was coming because I felt the energy. The room was completely silent, and then it happened.

It wasn't magic. I didn't turn into a wizard overnight.

It was gas.

Nothing but a huge fart in my stomach. My fart actually shook the room, and everyone laughed at me. Even the teachers laughed.

Ever since then people at school have called me Harry Farter.

Anyway, back to today. My birthday morning started off with hugs from Mom and Dad. After what happened last year my parents agreed I could stay home from school today, so the real discussion started at the breakfast table.

"So, what's your plan for today, Harry? Will you test yourself?" Mom asked.

"Why are you asking him to test himself? We all know by the end of the day he will automatically discover his powers. It runs in the family." Dad seemed pretty confident.

I knew this was just the beginning. My parents love to argue back and forth, but it's usually in a fun playful way so it doesn't bother me.

"It runs in the family!" Mom exclaimed. "Are you serious? You didn't even know about Harry's famous wizard cousin. I was the one who discovered it and named our son Harry so that one day he could be famous too!"

"Okay, okay. I agree. But, I 'm confident that our Harry will discover his powers today without any extra effort or embarrassing moments. I might not be a wizard, but many of my ancestors were." Dad was really proud about his family background.

"Well then, what stopped you from becoming one?" Mom asked.

"Love! It's the only reason."

"Love?"

"It all ends when we fall in love with gorgeous women who, although they don't have any wizard blood in their families, have the power to attract us men." Dad had a sarcastic smile on his face as he gave this explanation, and he gave Mom a wink from the corner of his eye.

"Oh, now I understand; you blame me. I mean, if Harry becomes a wizard today, you'll say it's because of your blood, and if he doesn't, you'll say it's because of my family."

"Mom! Dad! It's my birthday! Please don't spend the entire day arguing like this. It's only 7:30 AM, and we have the entire day to find out what happens. Let's just wait and see." I pleaded.

"Sure, Harry, but we'll need to have some alternatives ready in case your mom's blood turns out to be more powerful than mine," Dad was still being sarcastic.

"I have a backup plan that could actually turn out to be the greatest gift a mother can give her son."

"Really, Mom? What kind of plan?"

"Even if your wizard powers don't show up today, I still plan to enroll you in magic school."

"That's a nice idea, Mom, but I'm afraid it won't work. Muggles are not allowed to learn magic."

"I did some research and I found a few schools teaching wizardry that allow Muggles to join if we pay double the tuition."

"DOUBLE? How are we supposed to pay double tuition? Are they going to teach Harry how to grow money on trees?" Dad said.

"Don't be so dramatic. I know my son has wizardry in him, and I intend to try my best to let the world know about it, even if it costs us a lot of money. I've always believed that one day Harry will shine as brightly as his famous cousin and that day is coming very soon."

"We can discuss that later. For now, let's stop all this wizard talk and decide how we're going to celebrate Harry's eleventh birthday. Where's

Chris? She must have some ideas, too. Let's find out what she wants to do since she's staying home today as well." Dad went upstairs to wake Christina up.

Mom left to get the ingredients ready for my favorite chocolate ice-cream cake.

The rest of the day was a lot of fun; Paul and Shelly, my friends from next door, got out of school early so they came over to hang out with us. They were just as anxious as we were to find out whether my life would take a major turn on my eleventh birthday.

"Harry, when will it happen?" Shelly asked.

"When will what happen?"

"When will you turn into a wizard?"

"Shelly, to be honest, I don't really think I'll become a wizard today. But I definitely want to be one, so Mom has a plan ready for me if nothing happens today."

"Plan? What's the plan?"

"Moms never share their plans with kids, so don't ask him." Paul said.

I didn't want to go into detail so I kept quiet about Mom's plan. It was getting late, so Paul and Shelly decided to go home. I promised them that I would let them know if anything special happened.

We waited and waited, but nothing happened. Mom was anxious and disheartened at the same time, but Dad was still patient. He told Chris and me to go to bed, and said that we would talk about the next step in the morning.

The day might not have been too special, but the night was. Not in real life, but in my dream. A beautiful fairy touched me with her magic wand and said, "Harry, starting tomorrow, you will be a different person. You'll have powers like no other, but you'll have to discover them. The journey to discovery will be tough, but once you have made the journey, you will become the defender of your people."

I woke up startled and looked around. I remembered the dream so clearly that I thought I could reach out and touch the fairy from the dream. It felt so real that I actually did reach my hand out, but there was nothing there. When I dropped my hand back to my pillow, I noticed that something was underneath it. I pulled it out and saw that it was some kind of bottle.

At first, I thought it must be one of my water bottles, or one of Christina's, but why would it be under my pillow? As I looked more closely I didn't recognize it at all, and I was a little surprised to see a shiny green liquid inside it.

Unsure if I was actually awake or still dreaming, I rubbed my eyes, and stared at the bottle. I turned it around in my hands, trying to see if there was a label or instructions on it but I didn't see anything. Then I remembered a conversation I had had with my Mom earlier that day:

"My friend Sally has the most wonderful homemade potions, and I want you to try one of them, dear. You'll love it! It's your favorite color – green, and it's supposed to be really good for your stomach and helps prevent gas problems. We all remember what happened last year on your birthday!"

"Aw, Mom! I don't want to try any of your friend's crazy potions! You keep saying how great they are, but I've never seen you drinking any!"

Chuckling, she had replied "Sally makes special potions for me and I drink them every night, the reason no one knows is that I don't want anyone to discover my beauty secrets now, would I?"

My dad jumped in, "Kids, it's a good thing you and your sister aren't allowed to see your mom too early in the morning. Now you know the reason why. You wouldn't want to see her before she drinks her beauty potions! I love your mother, but I wouldn't recommend anyone see her before the makeup arrives on her face."

Mom threw a kitchen towel on the floor and stomped out of the room to go water her plants, leaving the rest of us laughing at Dad's joke.

I smiled at the memory as I opened the bottle, poured out the liquid in the bathroom sink, and threw it in the trashcan. I may have had a hard year and I'm trying to get rid of my Harry

Farter nickname, but green potion mixed by some crazy lady who makes beauty potions for my Mom? No, thank you. I went back to my bed, laid my head on my pillow and, in seconds, I was sleeping again.

Wednesday

I told my mom about my dream, and she told Chris and Dad about it. Everyone was happy, but, like me, they were not sure whether the dream had anything to do with real life.

After school, I decided to take Chris to the nearby park and try out some of the new moves I had practiced to beat her at soccer. She is surprisingly good at the sport; she even calls it football and can name over 100 professional players. Chris has a really strong kick and she can run fast for her age; Mom and Dad have actually been talking about getting her a private coach so that she can get even better and get a scholarship one day.

We were in the park in five minutes. Ten minutes after that I found myself lying flat on my back, completely out of breath. Chris was definitely getting better every day, and, of course, I was distracted with thoughts about becoming a wizard so I couldn't really keep up with her. One of our friends, Derek, was playing with us.

"Hey, Harry! Why are you laying on the ground like that? Are you going to let a girl beat you? Come on! Get up!"

"Derek, when are you going to learn that just because she's a girl doesn't mean she's weak! You know Chris is better than both of us."

"I get it, I get it. But look, we gotta beat your sister! We're playing 2 against 1 and we haven't scored a single goal. That's why I'm tryin' out different moves so she doesn't know where the ball's gonna go next."

"Dude, the way we're running around the field, it' like we're the ones who have no idea where the ball is going," I replied.

My Mom likes Derek; she sometimes calls him my "brother from another mother" because he's always at our house and we actually look pretty similar. Chris even has a little joke of her own about it.

"Harry, which one of you is supposed to be my older brother. You both stink at football, maybe I should call you my sisters?" I prayed that she never said anything in front of my other friends because it's embarrassing to have your younger sister be better than you at sports. Once I made the mistake of telling Derek what Chris said in front of one of the guys at school, Samuel Watson, and Samuel ended up rolling on the floor laughing.

Samuel, he preferred to be called Samuel and not Sam, was about two years older than me, and a really accomplished wizard. All the boys I knew wanted to be like him. Even my Mom sometimes asked me to learn a couple of things from Samuel (see, even Moms never dared call him Sam) so I could become a wizard faster. But there was something about him that didn't exactly sit right with me. I can't tell what it is, but I just don't like him.

After we played soccer, the only thing I had to show for it was a serious case of exhaustion. All of my running around had only improved Chris's confidence (she beat us 5-1). Derek said that he must have lost 5 pounds because his shirt was soaked with sweat. I guess at least the exercise is good for us – hopefully I'll sleep really good tonight.

As the three of us were about to leave the park I spotted Samuel. He had apparently been hiding behind the trees in the park and was now quietly sneaking away. Derek saw him at the same time so he looked at me,

"Is that Samuel spying on us? He probably wants to see if you're a wizard now or still plain old Harry Farter."

"Thanks, Derek! That's just what I wanted to hear today," I replied.

"Harry! You sound like Dad! Are you and Derek going to get married and argue like Mom and Dad?" Christina said.

"No, we're not getting married! Why don't you marry your stupid soccer ball since you're so good at it and leave us alone," Derek answered back.

They bickered for the next five minutes until we got close to home, then Derek headed towards his house in a different direction. I was feeling a little sad because I still didn't feel anything different. Would I ever really get to be a wizard?

On our way home, Chris kept making fun of me and Derek: "do you guys brush your teeth together? Do you talk to each other while you're in the bathroom? Maybe you guys should pay me for soccer lessons."

When we got home, something weird happened the moment I stepped inside the front door. I felt that same tingling feeling in my chest and stomach. This was the same feeling I had last year on my birthday, but I learned my lesson and I knew it didn't mean I was turning into a wizard. I told Mom about the feeling in my stomach.

"What did Derek make you eat? You look awful!"

"Nothing, Mom!"

"Drink more green potion and you should feel better by dinner time."

"Umm...I don't think I should drink any more of that potion; I'm sure I'll be fine."

I went to my room and plopped down on the bed. I got the anxious feeling again that my family and I were waiting for something to happen to prove that I had indeed turned into a wizard. So far, given the feeling in my stomach, it looks like all I can do is create jumbo size farts. I'm tired of people making fun of me and calling me Harry Farter. Then I remembered the dream. I reminded myself that I'm related to a famous wizard, so things have to work out for me, which made me feel better, and then I fell into a deep sleep.

Waking up a few hours later, I blinked in the dark and lay quietly for a few minutes. I was trying to figure out if anything about me felt different, but the only thing I felt was my bloated stomach.

I sat up and looked around my room. Something feels off, I can't tell what it is but it's making me feel uncomfortable.

I jerked my head around quickly because I heard a sound and I thought maybe someone was in my room. It was just the shadows shifting around as the wind blew through the trees outside my windows, I couldn't see anything else.

I still couldn't shake the feeling in my gut that something was wrong. Why did I just wake up in the middle of the night? I had that nervous feeling, almost like when everyone is watching you and you get really nervous you'll say something wrong and they'll laugh at your or, like in my case, you fart and become the laughing stock of the whole school.

Suddenly, there was a sound at the window – **PLOP!**

I got up and walked over the window, then I moved the curtain to see what happened.

Bird poop! How did so much bird poop get on my window!

This bad luck never ends.

Thursday

I woke up to the feeling of something pecking at my feet. I blinked my eyes and even before I could find out who, or what, was tapping my feet, I remembered the window incident last night and sat up in a hurry.

And then, there it was. Out of nowhere there was a small colorful bird standing at the foot of my bed. I love animals, and sometimes I feel like I'm able to understand them. Last year, while I was in the park in my neighborhood, I overheard two sparrow talking to each other.

"For the love of your white feathers, why do you have to clean them up so much? We're only visiting the neighbors' nest, not the Queen of England!"

A female voice replied, "Oh, be quiet! I saw what you did last night. You crept out of the nest in the middle of the night, nearly making me jump out of my feathers, and flew into the lake. I was wondering what in the world possessed you to go dunk yourself in those icy cold waters! And then, of course, I remembered, we're visiting the neighbors tomorrow." There was a lot of sarcasm towards the end.

"Oh, all right! I won't argue with you. But you already look so pretty!"

But wait! How did that even happen? I just realized for the past year I've been able to hear what animals are thinking or saying to eachother. Weird, all this time and I never really thought about it. That has to be a magic power!

Getting up from the bed in a fit of excitement, I was heading towards the bathroom when the little bird in my bed started flying around me. I sensed that he was also a little annoyed as if he were saying, "Hey, how about saying good morning?"

I stopped and stared hard at him and noticed a thin line of green feathers on his head. The bird looked really cool up close, and I decided to name him Hornet. "Good morning, Hornet! Is it okay if I call you Hornet? He seemed happy and flew around my head a couple of times before he went and sat on the windowsill. I guess I know who made that mess on my window last night!

I went to the bathroom and noticed I felt happier. I didn't know why I felt so light- hearted and optimistic, probably because I went to sleep feeling better about everything. I guess it's true, when I go to sleep sad or angry I wake up feeling the same way. This feels much better.

Staring into the mirror, I could see my small face, a little pinker than usual, looking back at me. I picked up my toothbrush and was about to squeeze some toothpaste on it when I noticed a little green line on my palm, just below my thumb.

At first I thought it must something from that green potion that I touched, so I rubbed my palm gently. But even after a couple of minutes, I could still see the line very clearly. I was even more surprised when Hornet flew onto my palm and settled himself calmly, and that's when I noticed that the line on his head was an exact match to the green line on my palm.

WHOA! Yes! It's a sign! Finally. This had to be the sign that I was waiting for! I was excited! Even Hornet seemed to be excited for me. I gently touched him and stroked the green line on his forehead, and the line in my palm started to glow. Amazing!

I knew about my famous cousin's brave and strong owl, but I didn't think they shared as strong a bond as I did with Hornet. I was about to drop everything and run towards the kitchen, then I realized I hadn't brushed my teeth yet.

I quickly finished freshening up, put on my clothes, and rushed to the kitchen where I knew my dad would be reading the newspaper while Mom would be drinking coffee, same as every morning.

"Mom, Dad! I got a sign!"

My Mom looked at me, gave me a huge hug and said, "I knew you were a true wizard and would give us this good news! So, what exactly happened? Tell me everything!"

My dad chimed in "Good going, son! Let's hear the story."

I started telling them about last night and this morning, and both of them gasped when they heard about the birth poop on my window. And then, right on cue, Hornet flew into the kitchen and sat down on my hand.

My parents were amazed, and they wanted to pet Hornet, but he was a little afraid of all the attention. I could hear him saying, "Hold on! I'm not a cat! Get too close and I'll bite your hand!" I told my parents about this and they backed off, they looked even more confused. My dad was the first to say something.

"Harry, are you telling me that you can hear what Hornet is thinking?"

"Yea, Dad. Come to think of it, ever since my birthday last year I've been able to hear birds and animals talk to each other. After I farted at school, I felt really embarrassed so I went to the park to get away from everything and I heard two sparrows talking to each other. I was so distracted with what happened at school that I didn't even realize I could do it."

My Mom was staring at me, she started crying (happy tears). I knew she loved everything in nature, and she was always talking about saving the environment and natural resources and stuff. She even travels around for work to go to conferences about saving the planet.

"Harry, this is wonderful! I could sure use your help at work. This is fantastic!"

My dad jokingly replied "Sweetheart, the next time we're driving down a country road, and a deer refuses to move, we should ask Harry to have a talk with it and ask them not to hold up traffic. Shall we go ahead and pack our bags for a trip now?"

"Stop it! Your jokes aren't even funny." Mom said.

"I have bigger plans than asking Harry here to just get animals to cross roads! Give me some credit! I'm going to get a host of pets now, and ask Harry to train them to get the morning paper, do your food shopping, maybe even get them to do the cooking and cleaning around the house!"

We all started laughing, and even Hornet seemed to be having a good time. He happily started jumping from one hand to the other, letting out small chirps.

And then suddenly, without warning, Hornet pooped in my hand.

"NOT IN MY HAND!" I said.

Hornet was so startled because I shouted and he fell out of my hand and onto the floor. My Mom and dad covered their mouths and looked like they were about to fall down themselves. I know they wanted to laugh. To make matters worse, my sister Chris walked into the kitchen right at the moment, she looked confused, wondering why I had so much bird poop in my hand.

Everybody stared at me. Then the doorbell rang.

Christina, ran towards the front door since she was the closest, while my parents looked at each other and started to laugh really loud. In fact, they were laughing so hard that they had to hold each other up – they almost fell over the breakfast table.

I ran toward the bathroom because I needed to wash my hand and I didn't want to see my parents laughing at me.

On the way back I passed the front door and I saw a strange woman standing there talking to my sister. Chris was looking at a piece of paper that the woman had given her so she didn't see me coming, but the woman saw me. She looked up suddenly and was staring into my eyes.

Right at that moment, I could feel Hornet standing on my shoulder, holding on tight with his feet. The green line on my palms was glowing now. The woman tried to look at my hand, so I put my arms behind my back. My Dad came up behind me and started talking to the woman. "Hello! Can I help you?"

I don't know what I was expecting, but the woman's voice startled me. "Oh, hello! I'm sorry – I seemed to have interrupted something hilarious," she said with a smile. I looked up at my dad and I noticed he was wiping away tears from his eyes, tears of laughter from what just happened.

"Just a little family humor, is all. So who are you?"

Chris spoke up, "Dad, she's our new neighbor and was introducing herself to me. She said she loves my dress and is a fashion designer. Look! Here is a dress that she drew on this piece of paper in less than thirty seconds!"

I was still looking at the woman, and at the same time I was praying that Hornet wouldn't poop on my shoulder. Not in front of strangers, please!

Mom came forward and said, "It's lovely to meet you. Please, why don't you join us for some breakfast or coffee? And I'm afraid we didn't catch your name."

The woman replied, "I'm Lucinda. Lucinda Marshall. I'll be living down the street and just came by to say a quick hello and introduce myself! I've already had breakfast, but thank you for the invitation!"

Mom and Dad were polite and talked to Lucinda for a few minutes at the door, but I noticed they seemed to be doing most of the talking while Lucinda was very quiet. I was getting uncomfortable, something isn't right and I wondered if my parents got the same feeling too. In a way, it was a lot like the uncomfortable feeling I get around Samuel.

The moment I started thinking about Samuel, I suddenly felt as if Lucinda had somehow read my mind and knew exactly what I was thinking. I looked up at her face and noticed she was facing my parents but her eyes were locked onto me. Suddenly I felt my hand throbbing behind my back. I stepped away to take a look at my hand and the green line was glowing bright green, brighter than a green traffic light!

After what seemed liked ages, Lucinda finally left, and we all went back to the breakfast table. I was still a little upset about that Hornet pooped on me; I need to figure out how to train him so that it doesn't happen again.

I decided to take a walk around the neighborhood and see if anyone could help me with tips about how to take care of him and what should I feed him. I put on my sneakers, told my parents I was going out for a bit, and then I was on my way.

Friday

When I opened my eyes in the morning, the memories from yesterday came rushing back to me. On the surface, it seemed like a regular day, but now I was pretty sure I was a wizard because I could feel small changes in me. The green line that glowed on my palm, Hornet, the way the green line lit up when we met Lucinda, and the way Lucinda looked at me when I thought about Samuel – seems like a lot happened to me in a short amount of time.

But, as with all people with magic in their blood, there were three things that I still had to take care of, by myself. These were certain tests that I had to take on my own, without any help, if I wanted to be 100% sure that I am, indeed, a wizard.

I was surprised that Mom hadn't asked me about them already. But I remembered that these were extremely personal tests and that no one could force me into them. When the time was right, I just had to tell my parents whether I had successfully passed them. I think I'll get started on them this weekend. I already know what the first two are but the third is supposed to a mystery. In other words, you don't know what the last test is until it shows up.

I ran into a group of guys on my way to school today. They were all confirmed wizards and were talking about their powers. One of them was able to change his voice to imitate anyone in the world, as long as he could hear them speak for a few seconds. It was amazing, he even imitates his Mom's voice and his Dad can't tell the difference, so he used it to get a bigger allowance. One of the other boys said he could fix anything mechanical, including cars and trucks! His parents said they never had to buy another car for the rest of their lives!

Then it was my turn. They all turned towards me, and someone asked, "Hey Farter, what can you do besides blow gas in your pants? Has your famous cousin taught you anything yet or are you still Harry Farter the loser?"

It's been over a year and people still remember me as the person who farted. It's really annoying! I wish they would move on already. I told them it's still early and my powers were developing, but for starters I could hear animals talk.

They thought I was joking so someone asked me to prove it.

I looked around and saw two cats walking around pretty close to us. The cats near school are actually dangerous.

There's a rumor they scratched one of the teachers really bad because she tried to close a window near one of them. I don't know if it's true, but everyone says they're dangerous and we're not allowed to go near them.

These cats didn't exactly look friendly. They both had long sharp claws and looked hungry. I tried to listen in to hear what they were talking about. Thankfully, I could just make out what one cat was saying to the other:

"Look at these annoying kids. They've been talking non-stop and they're scaring all the food away. I've had enough of this noise!"

"Hey, forget the noise. Look at that tasty bird sitting on that boy's shoulder. Isn't he the boy who farts?"

"Forget about that bird. Wouldn't want to get caught in one his monstrous farts," replied the first cat. Even though

I could hear them making fun of me, I had to look past it because everyone was waiting for me to prove I wasn't a liar.

"Let's ignore those noisy humans and find something to eat!" said one cat.

"Whatever you say," replied the second cat before they started to walk away.

I decided to focus on the less hungry looking cat, and spoke to him with my mind (I didn't even know I could do that until today, amazing!). "Hey! Cat! Can I convince you to walk over here and sit in front of me? I'm trying to prove to everyone here that I can communicate with you. I'll make it worth your while."

The cat looked at me with arrogant eyes and let out a really loud meow. He was getting his claws ready to make a move. Everyone was getting nervous, but nobody moved.

"Really! Aren't you a crazy one? What makes you think I would do that for you? Can't you see – I'm looking for food!"

I replied, again using only my mind, "Of course, that's exactly why if you help me out, I'll open the back door to the school kitchen – you can find plenty to eat there!"

The cat immediately walked over to us, arched its back and flicked its tail, all while staring directly at me. Then it turned around and sat down, facing the rest of the group. Everyone's jaw dropped. No one has ever been this close to one of these wild cats. I'm pretty sure they were all impressed. I was about to bend down to pet the cat when I heard it say:

"Uh-uh. Don't even think about touching me. I did as you asked, now go open that door for us you strange wizard."

I walked away to open the door for the cats, so I couldn't hear what everyone was saying. But either way, I'm the only person at school that can get near cats so that's pretty cool. Wait. Did the cat actually call me a wizard? So cats can differentiate wizards from Muggles?

After school I went home, had an early dinner with the rest of the family, and then I did my homework and went to bed. I like to do my homework on Friday; otherwise I forget and have to work on it Sunday night. I'd rather get it out of the way and then enjoy the weekend. What an awesome day!

Saturday

I was excited this morning. I whistled and Hornet came flying through the window and sat on my shoulder. I was petting him, but after a few minutes he started trying to eat my fingers and I remembered that I had to feed him. I did some research and learned that sparrows love eating corn, wheat, and oats so I keep a bag of food close by and whenever he's hungry I put some in a dish for him to eat.

Hornet was eating so I went to the bathroom to brush my teeth and I noticed the green line in my hand was dull. I figured out its some form of signal that warns me of danger! Once I finished cleaning up, I got dressed and whistled for Hornet. He flew over to me right away, I love when he does that! Now I'm ready for the first test.

I went down to the kitchen where everybody was already sitting at the breakfast table. They seemed to read the determination on my face and didn't say anything much to me. Mom and Dad continued talking about grown up stuff, and I was pretty sure they would start arguing soon, like they always do. Mom started saying she's adding more plants to her garden and that means more oxygen for the world, then Dad would say that half the water in the house was required to water her plants. Eventually they agreed there's enough water and more plants is a good thing.

I noticed Chris looking over at me from time to time while biting her nails, which meant she was thinking about something important. She gave me some of her toast and scrambled eggs because she knew I liked eating more from her plate than mine.

Once breakfast was over, I told everyone I was heading into town by myself to take care of something important. Dad stood up and got a serious look on his face. Mom looked a bit concerned. I started to get a little nervous now. Heck, I hadn't even started my first test!

Mom said something that surprised me, "Harry, there's a tradition that I told your dad to follow for you and your sister." She looked at Dad while she said this. "Your dad has been very smart this time and actually listened to me. You know all those chores you and Chris do around the house? Along with giving you both your normal allowance, we've been putting aside a small amount every week. We know that you will need the money that you have earned to pass some of your tests, so here you are."

She handed me a big glass jar that was full of money! I was so surprised, I couldn't even think of anything to say. Chris came over and hugged me, and all I could do was thank them. I said bye to everyone then I started to head into town.

I was really excited about my first test. The first step for any wizard is to create a wand. Things had changed quite a bit since my famous cousin just bought his wand at a store. I can't remember the name of the store but I know it starts with the letter 'O' and is hard to pronounce.

It seemed like a simple challenge but I was still all alone so it was a good amount of work for someone my age. Then I remembered something Dad told me once.

He said that the size of the person doesn't matter; it all comes down to your determination and what's inside you. Even though I was starting to get a little nervous about the challenges, I decided I had to keep going and face the first challenge head on.

Nowadays, a young wizard or witch has to earn everything, including their wands (and their pets), and my wand has to be created from scratch. I walked through the woods and found the tree where I had to pick some wood for my wand. This wasn't just any tree. This tree was special because the wood is supposed to be stronger than metal. I remember my uncle telling me bringing me here when I was only 5 years old. After all these years I never forgot about this tree, and I've been waiting for this day for a long time. So I had to collect the wood, and the wand maker would pick the right core, and help me create the wand that would be right for me.

I started looking carefully for just the right branch, nothing too flashy, and I couldn't just grab the first thing I came across. Luckily, this tree sheds wood every couple of months so I don't have to chop the branches off.

I found a sturdy piece of wood, but noticed that it was a little old, so I looked around for over an hour and collected a few more pieces that looked like they were strong, but still flexible and young.

I walked towards Roody's (Mr. Roody, the owner of the shop, always jokes that Woody's would've probably been a better name for his store). I opened the door, and went up to the counter where Mr. Roody was helping some other witches and wizards with their wands. I was a little nervous and wanted to attempt my first test on my own, without an audience, so I went to sit in a chair a little away from the counter and tried my best not to listen to what was happening back there.

Mr. Roody continued to help the other people there but he looked impatient. One of the boys had ended up sticking the wand in his mouth to bite it and now there were flashing lights and sparks coming out of his stomach. The girl was looking at him and laughing out loud, while her own wand was flying around uncontrollably and she was unable to grab it.

Finally, Mr. Roody helped stop the sparks in the boy's stomach and he taught the girl how to handle her wand. They eventually paid and left the shop. Finally, it was my turn.

"Hello, Mr. Roody."

"Hello, young man. It's Harry, isn't it?" I nodded with a smile.

"Well, I think I know why you're here. It looks like your time has come; have you collected the material you want your wand to be made of?"

I laid down the wood that I collected on my way to the shop and Mr. Roody exclaimed "Ah, secret oak! A wise choice. And I see that you've collected a few tender green saplings like some of our earlier friends had chosen, but you've also included fully matured pieces of wood that are still flexible and are just perfect to make strong and brilliant wands. Let's get started, shall we?"

This was it, pretty soon I would have my own wand! I suddenly realized the green line on my palm was glowing softly again. Was it because I was nervous? I feel something in my stomach too. I hope I don't fart.

I watched as Mr. Roody worked his own magic on the piece of wood he thought was the best of the bunch. He'd gathered a few things on his table: a feather, a few drops of some ruby red liquid, a talon, a sabre's tooth (I think that's what it was), a few small plants with the leaves, and a bunch of other things.

I lost track of time. Mr. Roody was working on my wand and I couldn't keep up with what he was doing. I started thinking about all those kids at school that call me names. Harry Farter, Farter Boy, Harry Farter the loser, sometimes people at school can be really mean. I try not to think about it, but it still bothers me every once in a while. I'm looking forward to having my wand so that I can prove I'm a wizard. I wonder if I can turn things around so that they fart whenever I point my wand at them. That would be cool!

Mr. Roody turned towards me and said he was almost done. He handed me the piece of wood, and I held it in my hand and swished it a little, but nothing happened. Apparently, it was not easy to create the perfect wand on the first try.

He took the wand back and made a few adjustments, then handed it back to me. Still, nothing happened.

The third time he did this, the piece of wood in my hand immediately transformed into a long, thick, highly polished, gold-tipped wand. I could see an inscription in gold at the bottom of the wand, just where I was holding it. The inscription included my initials, a date and time stamp, and a few other abbreviations that I couldn't understand. I was still the only person in the shop, so Mr. Roody had some time to spare.

"Harry, your wand is a special one. The way you selected the wood showed that you have solid common sense. You may make mistakes, but you have the potential and strength to correct them yourself. There's a hidden quality in you that shows you have a desire to help, not only yourself, but also others around you as well.

"Your wand's core is a mixture of three elements, instead of the usual two that are used in most other wands. One is from a special young plant; the second element is a mixture of fairy dust and crushed rose petals; and, lastly, the rarest of all, powdered scale from one of the fiercest dragons that have ever roamed this planet."

"Why is the last ingredient a rare one, Mr. Roody?"

"Harry, I've been making wands for about 70 years now, of which the last five years have been devoted to adding cores to wands. In all these years, I've only used dragon scales seven times, and today would be the eighth. Dragons are powerful beasts who can be the most ferocious when angered, but the most loyal, one of the most intelligent, and one of the most useful creatures that have ever roamed this planet. "

This sounded expensive. I'm glad Mom and Dad gave me that jar full of money. Mr. Roody continued talking.

"So your wand is a combination of love of nature and softness because your wand chose the young plant, pure magic because of the fairy dust and rose petals' mixture, and great strength and ferocity because of the dragon scale. I believe you will be involved in some very interesting events, and I'm sure you will persevere."

I was surprised that I was considered worthy of having a special wand, and I knew I was never going to part with it. I loved the way the gold tips and inscription complemented the dark brown wood.

I paid Mr. Roody and thanked him for his help and explanation. I was about to leave when I saw Samuel through the window. It looked like he was spying on me and was trying to sneak away from the shop. I instantly felt uneasy.

I was heading home with my wand under one arm and Hornet on my other shoulder when suddenly the green line on my palm started glowing bright green. I knew something was wrong and I was about to start running when I saw that the bush next to me was on fire. I was shocked – I couldn't figure out how it caught fire because I was standing right there, and nobody else was in sight!

Hornet was flying around my head and then shot off as if he was chasing something. I followed him with my eyes and saw that Samuel was running away as fast as he could.

Then, I suddenly remembered what Samuel's power was: the ability to create fire. He was capable of making pretty much anything burst into flames. He also had the power to glide over the ground for short distances, which made him a really powerful wizard. Speed and fire were a very powerful combination, and dangerous. But why did he have to set the bush near me on fire? Now I was angry.

Hornet came flying back, even more agitated than usual. I knew he thought of himself as my guardian angel, and he felt he had somehow let me down because he didn't warn me of the danger. I pet him was able to calm him down. We kept walking home, now I'm positive Samuel is up to no good!

****

Mom was really happy when I showed her my new wand and I told her about Mr. Roody. I didn't say anything about the fire or about Samuel.

I heard voices in the living room, and I saw that Lucinda Marshall was chatting with my sister Chris. Again, I felt uneasy, and my new wand grew a little warm in my hand while the green line was glowing brightly. Mom, too, was instantly alert. Now that we all knew the green line in my hand signals danger, she looked around to see what it could be and we both found ourselves staring at Lucinda. She was, after all, the only stranger in our house.

Lucinda realized we were staring at her because she suddenly stopped smiling. I was wondering what she was about to do when suddenly, we could all hear my Uncle Frank's voice shouting at the front door. Now everyone knew that there was definitely some kind of trouble brewing. Uncle Frank was banging hard on the door, my entire hand was green at this point, and Hornet was flying around crazily. It was a mess. Chris seemed to be watching all of this in a daze.

I managed to open the front door and, as soon as Lucinda saw who it was, she got up and jumped out of the open window. Hornet flew after her. I couldn't believe she just jumped out of the window and I had to blink a few times to make sure I wasn't dreaming. I looked at Uncle Frank, whose random appearance was only a little less crazy than Lucinda's exit.

Uncle Frank is my dad's wizard brother, and one of our richest and quietest relatives. He was generally loved by everyone in the family and lived peacefully in a mansion far away from us. He doesn't have any kids, and he's really nice to Chris and me (he gives us a lot of presents). We usually go visit him when we're on summer break from school.

"Frank! What on earth are you doing here all of a sudden? And why did our neighbor jump out the window the minute she saw you? What is going on?" Mom was yelling.

He started talking to Mom then he suddenly shouted:

"Look at Chris!"

We looked and saw that she was lying unconscious on the couch. We ran over and tried waking her up. Her forehead was damp and she felt hot, as if she had a fever. Uncle Frank gently lifted her head and put his hands behind her neck. I was scared, Chris is my sister and something like this never happened in real life. I don't know what I would do without her and I just hoped she would be ok.

Uncle Frank inspected her eyes, ears and mouth to make sure she was breathing. He told us that she would be okay. He said Lucinda tried putting a spell on her, but fortunately she hadn't been able to complete her spell and the effects would wear off in a little while. He asked Mom to put Chris to bed, and then come join us when done.

Mom came back to the living room and sat down. Then Uncle Frank looked at me and he began explaining what was going on:

"Harry, I understand you've cleared your first test today and now you have an exceptional wand. Which is wonderful, Congratulations! Now, as you know, you can't actually use the wand until you pass the second test. I suspect Lucinda and her son Samuel knew about this and that's why they moved their attack a day ahead."

"Uncle Frank, I don't understand what you're trying to say. I got my wand today, and yes, I know I still have to face a second test. But what's this about Lucinda and Samuel? They're not mother and son! Her last name is Marshall and his is Watson. And what attack are you talking about?"

"Harry, I'm afraid that, now that you're becoming a full-fledged wizard, you're going notice you have some enemies out there. Lucinda is capable of brain washing Muggles, and she's one of the most expert potion makers in the world. Samuel has the gift of speed and fire, as you probably ready know.

Actually, Lucinda is his stepmother; his father married a second time after Samuel's mother passed away six years ago. Lucinda was living in Essex back then, but she had to leave in a hurry because I found out about her evil plans."

"What evil plans?" Mom shouted. "And what happened to Chris?"

"She was in the process of putting a spell on Chris so that she would be able to control her mind. I think she was planning use Chris to lure Harry over to her and Samuel so that they could take him away. She knows Harry would never follow her and Samuel on his own.

You see, I've known about Lucinda for sometime now. She managed to have a very dangerous weapon approved for development by brainwashing a defense contractor who lives in Essex. The weapon combines the powers of one of her deadliest potions and Samuel's skill with fire.

"She approached me once and tried to convince me to approve the weapon plan (uncle Frank was a Director in the Armaments' division for military forces because he loved spending time with

Muggles and wanted to understand weapons better. He'd always said that that the more you knew about something, the less dangerous it could be for you in the future), but I saw right through her and threatened to inform the Magical Powers' Governance Council, along with the Muggle authorities.

"Unfortunately, she was able to convince another defense director, a Muggle, to approve her plans, because she used her powers to take control of his mind."

I was still puzzled about how we fit into the picture when uncle Frank continued:

"Lucinda and Samuel were planning to finalize the weapon here, but he had been watching you, Harry, and told his stepmother about your potential powers. Unlike the other kids at school who give you a hard time, Samuel actually knows you have the potential to be the most powerful wizard in school because of your famous cousin, but he convinces the other kids at school to call you names to distract everyone from seeing your true potential.

"You see, fire is an element of nature, and you now have control over other natural elements, such as birds and animals, and possibly even wind and water. That's a potential threat to their plans, and Lucinda wanted to put you out of the picture until her plan was finalized and she became one of the wealthiest and most powerful witches in the entire world.

"She planned to put a spell on Chris and use her to force Harry to agree to do as she said. Thank goodness Harry sensed the danger and spotted Samuel earlier today. Samuel was planning to attack Harry while he was on his way home from the wood shop."

Mom and I sat there, stunned. Just then, Dad walked through the door and he listened as uncle Frank explained what had happened and what was going on. Dad was angry and concerned about Chris, and asked uncle Frank what we should do next.

"I need you both to take Chris away to my mansion, which is well guarded and protected with enchantments. I'll shield you with spells so you all will be camouflaged and protected while traveling. Tomorrow, once Harry clears his second test, he and I will take on Lucinda and Samuel together."

My parents reminded uncle Frank that I was just an 11-year-old boy who had only very recently recognized his wizardly skills. But Uncle Frank convinced them that he would protect me as if I were his own son. I'm glad my uncle Frank is a powerful wizard, otherwise, we would be in trouble.

It was getting late so we all started going to bed. Uncle Frank asked me to wake up really early so that I could clear my second test first thing tomorrow morning. After that, the rest of my family would head to his mansion. Hornet was pretty calm, so I asked him to wake me up early in the morning (Hornet always wakes up early). He disappeared for a while after he had chased Lucinda, but now he was back and he didn't leave my side while I slept that night. Uncle Frank slept in the guest room, and he set his alarm for 5:00 AM so that he could check on me in the morning.

Sunday

Hornet woke me up at 4:45 AM, and I realized more than ever how urgent it was for me to clear my second challenge. The second test required me to stare into a fire and look for images of the future. I went outside to the back yard, keeping my wand beside me, and got a nice fire going. Dad had taught me how to build a fire. It's dangerous though, so I don't do it often and I make sure someone is close by just in case it gets too big for me to handle.

I looked into the flames and instantly was able to see a massive weapon with the wavy figures of Lucinda and Samuel behind it. It looked like they were adding finishing touches to it, and they were rushing to get it done. That was easy. I'd cleared my second test with flying colors, but now I was terrified by what I saw.

I was about to run back inside when uncle Frank came rushing out and asked me what I saw. "How much time do we have?" he asked.

"Not much," I replied, "the weapon is almost ready."

Uncle Frank rushed toward the rest of family who were already up and dressed for the ride back to uncle Frank's mansion. Uncle Frank promised me that they would be fully protected and nothing would happen to them while they were on their way.

I don't know what made me do it, some kind of impulse, I guess, but I lifted my wand and swirled it around everyone, wishing with all my heart that they would remain safe while they were away. The air began to swirl around the room as my wand moved, and my family was encircled by a bright, golden bubble for a few seconds before it faded away.

I really am becoming a wizard! Now I felt reassured that I had done my bit to keep my family safe.

Uncle Frank and I started walking toward Lucinda's house, where four other wizards (uncle Frank's friends) were waiting for us. We all listened to uncle Frank.

Uncle Frank's plan was simple; he had chosen this small group of wizards specifically because they had fire-resistant powers. They were to go after Samuel while uncle Frank and I combined our powers in an attack on Lucinda. We all stood in a circle, hidden from the house, and Uncle asked me if I was ready. I nodded yes.

He then turned towards the front door and blew it open with his wand. Uncle Frank's power was lightning and force, watching him use the power was awesome!

The four wizards immediately went after Samuel and they put up shields to block his fire. His power was useless and he couldn't outrun 4 wizards because they blocked him in every direction.

Hornet kept Samuel from fighting back by pecking at his face. When Lucinda saw us she turned to run, but I was ready this time.

I lifted my wand at the same time uncle Frank did. A bright red flame shot out of my wand and merged with the dark grey beam that shot out of uncle Frank's wand. Instantly, Lucinda was tied up in chains. Ha! Take that, creepy neighbor.

Samuel was also completely useless because he was no match for four experienced, fire-resistant wizards. The next thing I knew, four guards instantly appeared (there was so much magic I had to learn) and they took Lucinda and Samuel away – through thin air. Uncle Frank told me this was called tele-transportation.

The other wizards patted me on the back and told me I have a lot of potential and I did a great job for such a young age. They said other wizards my age would have been afraid and probably run away. Then one of them told me Samuel got scared and started crying when they approached him. I guess he's not so tough after all.

Uncle Frank took me back to my house where his car was. We were going to drive back to his mansion and meet my family there, so we had a long trip ahead of us.

Monday

We woke up early and got everything in the car so that we could head to Uncle Frank's mansion. As uncle Frank was driving, he looked at me and said, "Oh Harry, don't forget you still have one more challenge to complete. Unlike the first two challenges which are pretty easy, and you knew exactly what they were ahead of time, no one can tell you what the final challenge is, but you'll know it when you see it. Don't be afraid, I'm sure you will do fine. But there's a chance you could fail the final test and know as a farting muggle forever!"

"How do you know about that?" I asked.

"I'm sorry Harry, but everyone knows. I know you've had a rough year with people calling you names at school because of the incident. The good news is, if you clear the last challenge you'll be able to change that forever. Maybe even wipe it from everyone's memory."

That was good news! But I was amazed. How did Uncle know so much? My shock must've shown on my face because he went on to say, "Don't worry, I was afraid of my final challenge too! But guys like us don't cry when we're afraid, leave the crying for that Samuel Watson kid."

We both laughed and I felt a little relived, it was good to have someone like uncle Frank in the family. We kept driving toward his mansion.

Suddenly, the green line in my palm started glowing bright green. There was a big explosion next to our car so we had to stop; my ears were ringing from the noise. I got out of the car and looked in front of me. I couldn't believe what I saw. This was it. My third and final challenge was right here in front of me.

End of Book 1

About Wimpy Fart

Hey kids,

Want to tell Wimpy Fart what you think about this book?

Send an email!

(Parents can email Wimpy Fart too in order to find out when the next book will be available)

WimpyFart@gmail.com

Wimpy Fart Books is a small; family owned company dedicated to writing silly, fun to read books for kids.

Printed in Great Britain
by Amazon